RUMBLETUM

a.k.a. 'CANCER'

Written & illustrated by **Tony White**

Dedication

To all those special *'RUMBLETUM'* souls
who are born between late June and late
July!

*(And for my wife, daughters, grandkids, and great grandkids
– who are all very special to me!)*

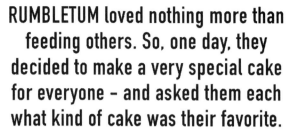

RUMBLETUM loved nothing more than feeding others. So, one day, they decided to make a very special cake for everyone – and asked them each what kind of cake was their favorite.

...as it preferred to have two different tastes at once.

So, 'Dark Chocolate Truffle Cake' best fitted the bill for them.

So they admitted that 'Multigrain Carrot Cake' was their favorite.

So, they chose 'Coconut Cake'.

'Victoria Sponge Cake' was their favorite.

DAYDREAM wanted something that was totally out of this world.

So, they chose 'Angel Food Cake'.

All this put RUMBLETUM in a very difficult position of course.

They all wanted different things, so how could they make everyone happy?

RUMBLETUM pondered for some time over all this.

"Something to please everyone!"

When RUMBLETUM was finished,
they showed it to the others.

It was a HUGE cake that was made-up of 12 parts — one for each of their favorite choices!

RUMBLETUM was very happy to see them all tuck in to the cake — although they were most pleased by the little, favorite cupcake that they had made for themselves!

ABOUT RUMBLETUM

RUMBLETUM represents the 4th Sign of the Zodiac, 'CANCER'. Aries is the first Sign of the 12 – a sensitive and nurturing energy that is said to reflect certain traits within the human personality. Yet it would be ridiculous to suggest that any one person can be defined as any one Birth Sign energy alone. Astrologically, we are each a combination of many diverse energies – in addition to much, much more outside of astrological thought. However, there is now doubt that individuals born at a certain time of the year tend to display some of the traits that their Birth Sign is thought to represent – some more and some less, depending on many things. Nevertheless, it might be fun to look at any of the 'RUMBLETUM/CANCER' individuals you know – born between the end of June and the end of July each year – to see if they reflect, in general, any of the following…

"Cancerians are the naturally MATERNAL types of the Zodiac, deeply feeling the need to FEED and NURTURE others. They are SENSITIVE to CHANGING MOODS and ENVIRONMENTS and will often protect their sensitivity to a threatening world by creating a HARD SHELL of apparent toughness around themselves. INTUITIVE and often PSYCHIC, Cancerians are aware of their need for SELF PROTECTION and will therefore totally immerse themselves in HOME matters (on the principle that an individual's home is their castle). The Sign of Cancer is ruled by the MOON."

*(Taken from the author's introductory book to astrology, "**Birth Chart**', also available on Amazon.)*

ABOUT THE AUTHOR

At birth, **Tony White** had multiple planets in Virgo, a Moon in Capricorn, with Sagittarius Rising. His Mars in Cancer was square Neptune in his 10th House, so he had great imagination and dreams for his work, albeit somewhat unfocused. He has had a successful career as award-winning animator. author & teacher, with a serious passion for metaphysics, spirituality, and mysticism in his private life. That life was transformed as a young teenager. when his eyes were opened to a higher form of evolutionary astrology by the remarkable Irish herbalist/astrologer. Samuel H. Weir. Tony has since proven the value of such knowledge repeatedly in his own life and career. He created his **STAR*TOONZ** characters many decades ago. initially under the name of the 'Supastars'. They later evolved into the characters you see here. Tony also animated the **STAR*TOONZ** - to provide unique and personal Birth Chart videos for friends & clients. Now. Tony now brings his reinvented Zodiac characters to the publishing world - by way of a series of black & white coloring books and complimentary, full-color Kindle edition. A new **STAR*TOONZ** story will initially be published privately - for subscribers - each month on Substack - https://substack.com/@hippydippyguru - then more publicly via Amazon. as indicated above. For further details. visit our website.

www.hippydippyguru.com

A color guide for all 12 **STAR*TOONZ** can be found here...
www.hippydippyguru.com/coloring.html

Made in the USA
Columbia, SC
06 August 2024

40076644R00024